SPEC

Moira MacDonal
work, patience, and support. And as always, to you, the reader.

FOR DAD

"And he suddenly knew that if she killed herself, he would die. Maybe not immediately, maybe not with the same blinding rush of pain, but it would happen. You couldn't live for very long without a heart."

- Jodi Picoult

GRANT JOLLY

THERE IS A PATH FROM YOUR HEART TO MINE

THE CRYSTAL MAN

GRANT JOLLY

THE CRYSTAL MAN

1

The man across the room was staring at me, right into my eyes. I felt as though he knew something I didn't. He was frail and his skin sagged like latex. I had already been in hospital for three days and he hadn't left his bed once.

There was never any family or friends sitting around his

bed at visiting time, which was a shame; nobody should be alone in such a horrible place. I questioned how much of that dear old man was left. He never spoke, nothing, not a peep; just sat there all day long, staring. On a rare occasion, his eyes would wander around the room, and then he would fall asleep.

I hate everything about hospitals. First of all, the smell makes me queasy; it's like a mix of antiseptic and death. You can almost feel illness entering your body as you inhale. Secondly, the food is revolting and it should be illegal in my opinion. Dried up mince, part-boiled potatoes and mushy peas? No thank you.

I try my hardest to stay healthy, to keep myself away from places like this. You can understand then, why I was furious to find myself in the coronary ward.

I have never smoked a day in my life and have only ever been drunk once, when I was eighteen; I was sick for three days after and that was enough to put me off it for the rest of my life. So how the hell did I end up in hospital, waiting to receive a heart transplant? Genetics.

Restrictive Hypertrophic Cardiomyopathy. I think that's what they called it. A rare heart disease. They said I could die suddenly. This was a hereditary disease, which meant no matter how healthy I was, it would have probably been the same outcome anyway.

Translated into English, the muscles in my heart had thickened so much, that sometimes I found it hard to breathe, amongst other things. The chest pains were sudden. Every time I felt one of those awful darts of pain shooting through my body, I thought I was going to croak it. The palpitations were just as horrible, they made me sweat like crazy; sometimes they made me dizzy and faint, other times I spewed my guts.

I basically sat around for two years waiting for someone to die. Luckily for me, someone eventually did and she was a perfect match. As sad as this made me feel, I was extremely grateful for the second chance that had been handed to me and I was determined to make the most of my life from then on, all going well.

It was the morning of the operation. I opened my eyes,

and old Bill was already staring at me. I smiled, though the sad expression on his face never changed.

I had bought new pyjamas and slippers for the operation, so I made my way into the bathroom and put them on. I felt fresh and ready. Although I was terrified of going under the knife, I just couldn't wait for the whole thing to be over. I could not wait to get back to my life.

A young nurse with blonde hair entered the room. But as she approached my bed, old Bill started going crazy. I don't know what brought it on, but he became hysterical, waving his hands around and screaming; this was the most movement I had seen him making since I'd got there. He just kept on screaming 'No!' and pointing at me. A few moments passed before another, older nurse ran into the room and stuck a needle in poor Bill's arm. He conked out almost immediately. The nurse stroked his head a little and then left.

"What was that all about?" said the young nurse.

"Beats me," I said as I climbed back onto the bed. She started to wheel me away.

"Are you ready for the big day, Charlie?" she smiled as I looked up at her.

"As ready as I'll ever be."

"You'll be fine, just fine. I promise."

The corridors seemed narrower than they had ever been before. I felt a little claustrophobic, but I tried not to panic too much. The way I looked at it, I could die waiting for a heart and I could also die during the operation. What did it matter?

The overhead fluorescent lights were bright as I

floated down the corridors. I counted the lights to calm myself and it worked. I was at twenty-six when we approached an elevator. The doors pinged open and we entered. A moment later and the doors pinged open again. After a few more corridors and a few more elevators, we were in theatre.

There were at least six surgeons standing there, waiting eagerly to carve me up like a Christmas turkey. I could never have been a surgeon; I just don't have the stomach for it. However, I have great respect and I am thankful for the people who do.

I couldn't really comprehend what they were telling me about the procedure. It was as though they were speaking a completely different language. I let them talk and I nodded every few seconds, pretending I understood. All I knew was that I needed a heart, and they were about to bless me with one.

The anaesthetist sat waiting, saying,

"Count down from thirty for me, Charlie."

And I did. When I was at twenty-eight, she placed a clear mask over my face; the gas knocked me out by the time I got to twenty-four. I call it the 'strawberry fuzz' because to me, the gas tastes like strawberries and makes your head feel fuzzy before you drift off to sleep. Simple.

I usually get panicky just before I drift off, but not this time, though I do recall something very peculiar.

I got the overwhelming feeling that I was not alone. Yes, the medical team were bustling about in the room, but I sensed that someone was watching over me. Now, looking back, it makes me shiver to the core, for the last thing I remember before the strawberry fuzz took me, was seeing a dark shadow leaning over my bed. At the time I thought it could just have been the anaesthesia messing with my head, but as it turns out - it wasn't.

After I became unconscious, the surgeons were to go to work on me by first cutting into my breastbone to access the heart. They then jacked me in to a heart-lung bypass machine which helps the blood circulate properly. After the new heart was hooked up, they restarted it and when it started pumping on its own, they got me off the bypass machine and sewed me up with wire. Apparently the wire has to stay there for the rest of your life. The operation took about six hours in total. I was then transported back through the claustrophobic corridors and into the intensive care unit. I didn't become conscious until the next morning and was only breathing with the help of a ventilator machine. It was loud and freaked me out a little and if I am entirely honest, I was just waiting for it to fall silent and for me to begin choking; luckily that never happened. I was soon breathing on my own. They said the operation had been a success and I would be able to go home in three to four weeks. Full recovery would take at least six months.

I was soon back in my old ward, but something was different. Old Bill's bed was empty and made up to perfection. The bed looked so lonely without him in it. I was expecting to wake up and find Bill staring at me with those old wrinkled eyes. As it turns out, he had died when I was in surgery. The thought of him dying alone saddened me and I hoped that I would not turn out like that, staring with vacant eyes, dying alone. I said a little prayer for Bill in my mind.

After long days of recovering in bed, I was at last able to get up and walk about. I was also allowed a coffee, so I made my way down the corridor to the 'Klix' machine; it wasn't Starbucks or even Costa, but it would have to do. It tasted like mud, but I was still grateful for the warm beverage as it passed my dry lips. And that's when I saw her.

She had the most beautiful big eyes you have ever seen. They were that wonderful colour, halfway between blue and green, almost grey, with those dark rings around the outside of her irises. Her hair was smooth, black and short; I think they call it a pixie-cut. There I was, alone in the corridor, sipping on cheap coffee and shuffling around like a hobo; and there she was, strolling down the corridor towards me, looking like an angel.

As she got closer I could feel butterflies beginning to stir in my gut. Then I realised, she too was about to indulge in a warm beverage. She looked at me and smiled; her lips were plump and red. I could now see that she was prettier than I had first thought, her skin was flawless. And then she spoke.

"That stuff any good?"

I hesitated,

"Eh...it tastes like mud."

She laughed,

"Maybe I should just save my money then?"

Her presence was making me nervous and I could feel myself beginning to sweat. I was never good in situations like these...probably the main reason I was single when I thought about it.

"Well, it's not gourmet, but I suppose it is consumable."

"Consumable will have to do. The coffee machine downstairs in my ward is out of order."

She moved in closer. I realised I was in the way. As I tried to move we did that dancing thing. You know, when you are in the street and you almost walk into someone, but don't quite bump and then you do the stupid penguin thing for a minute? Anyway, it made me feel awkward.

"Sorry."

She laughed again. This time

I joined in, with a nervous chuckle. She popped the coins into the slot and pressed 'E2'. The machine came alive and churned the coffee out into a plastic cup. She picked it up and took a cautious slurp.

"You're right, it DOES taste like mud."

We shared another giggle together and then she reached out her hand.

"What's your name? I'm Alice."

"Charlie. Nice to meet you."

Her hand was warm and I never wanted to let it go. I wondered just how long a handshake can go on before it becomes creepy or weird? I concluded about 2-3 seconds is fine, give or take.

"So what happened to you, how'd you end up in here?" For a moment I had almost forgotten I was in hospital.

"I had a bum ticker. They just gave me a new one." Alice seemed shocked.

"A heart transplant at your age? What are you, in your late twenties?"

I wondered if that was an intended compliment, you know, the way people are not sure about your age so they always go younger, just in case you get offended.

"I'll take that as a compliment. I am thirty-two. Although, right now I feel more like sixty-two."

"How was it? How are you feeling now?"

I hadn't really thought about it much until that moment.

"I feel pretty rough; it's only been a week or so. I guess it will take a while to get back to normal."

I started thinking about the new organ in my chest; it made me feel nauseous, so I changed the subject.

"Why are you here?"

Alice opened her red dressing

gown, lifted her pyjama top a little, and pulled at the waistband of the bottoms,

"My appendix burst."

"That's nasty. You are lucky you got to hospital in time. That could've killed you."

She smiled.

"I know, I guess I have someone up there on my side, watching over me."

Alice took another sip of coffee.

"I guess so," I said.

"I suppose you don't smoke then?"

I didn't know if that was a joke, but I think it was.

"No, no, never smoked a day

in my life," I said...

"Well don't start whatever you do, it's a bitch of a habit to quit. I'm going outside for a smoke, I'll see you around."

Alice shook my hand again.

"Yeah, nice meeting you."

"You too, Charlie."

She smiled that amazing smile again and then she disappeared; consumed by the long narrow corridors.

2

Alice was only in the hospital for a couple of days before she was allowed to go home. But in those few days we got to know each other a little better. She would wander away from her ward and up to the coronary ward to visit me. We would walk down to the old rickety coffee machine and drink some 'consumable' coffee. We shared funny stories from our childhoods and laughed. We also talked about the latest films, books, music. In fact, there wasn’t much we didn't talk about.

The thing is, it wasn't just small talk. We had a hell of a lot in common; we both had a passion for French cinema and horror films, we both liked the same directors, the same writers, the same musicians; the list goes on and on.

The nicest thing was the fact that I generally hadn't many people around to talk to, and I could recognise that the people I did talk to only wanted to know me for my money; I'll get to that later. My point is, Alice saw me for who I really was, and she liked me; I didn't tell her about the money.

Anyway, I guess you could say we became friends. I was sad the day she went home. I was glad she was healthy and feeling better, but the selfish part of me wanted her to stay, just a little bit longer. We traded phone numbers and e-mail details and she promised to stay in touch.

A few weeks passed before the doctor gave me the all-clear. I missed Alice and I was more than ready to go home. The hospital food was beginning to make me feel sick every time I took a bite. I could hardly think about it without gagging.

All of my stuff was packed. I just had to wait for the doctor coming round to sign me off and give me my medication, the medication I would be on for the rest of my life - those pills and the massive scar on my chest were a small price to pay to cheat death.

I was sitting in one of those plastic chairs they put out for visitors, waiting patiently, when I heard footsteps coming down the corridor. I looked at my watch: 14:00, right on time.

Dr Harper appeared in the doorway. He was the doctor who had been keeping an eye on me. He was a short stumpy fellow with a big round belly. His hair was grey and wispy and he wore a pair of old fashioned steel-rimmed glasses.

"How are we today, Mr Finch?" he said as he walked into the room.

"I'm feeling fine, looking forward to getting back to normality."

He picked up the chart at the end of my bed and rubbed

his plump stubbly chin.

"I can imagine. Well, everything looks good, I have no problem with signing you off."

I was so happy to hear those words; I had almost forgotten what the outside world looked like. Harper replaced the chart.

"Thank you," I said.

"Now, Mr Finch, there are a few things I have to go over with you first."

He was holding a box of pills, shaking them like a packet of Tic-Tacs.

"As you probably know, you must take this medication. It

is vital you do not forget." He was talking about Tacrolimus, an immunosupressant which would stop my body from attacking my new heart and ultimately stop the heart from being rejected.

"Don't worry, I'll remember. My life depends on it, right?" It was a lighthearted joke, but it didn't go down too well with the doctor.

"This is no joke, Charlie, you need to take this stuff." I wished I had kept my mouth closed. I just wanted to get out of there and be done with it.

"I'm sorry, I was only

fooling. I know how important the drugs are."

Harper raised his bushy eyebrows,

"Good. Now there is a leaflet inside the box, I suggest you give it a good read over. If you begin to experience any side effects, any whatsoever, call your doctor."

"Okay, I give you my word."

"And remember, you need to make the follow-up appointments with your local surgery."

"I will."

"Well, that's it then, any questions?"

"Nope, all good."

And that was that. I called a taxi and it arrived ten minutes later to take me home.

Although I was out of the hospital, I was far from recovered - full recovery would take months. Yeah, I could walk, talk and eat solid food, but I was still sore all over and had to take my time walking. I had strict instructions from Harper to take it easy; no heavy lifting or bending, and that was fine with me.

The ride home was relaxing. I stared out of the window, at nothing, and everything. The world seemed different, looked different. I felt as though I had been reborn with fresh eyes and there was a feeling of excitement in my gut. But I wondered if I would ever get used to the strange sensation of having a dead person's heart inside my chest. For the time being, everything was perfect and I tried not to dwell on the thought too much. *Renovatio*

Half an hour passed before I was home. My back was beginning to ache and I could not wait to get out of the taxi. The driver pulled into my driveway and got as close to the front door as he possibly could. I was excited and paid promptly, with a considerable tip. I grabbed my bag, said thanks and left, pushing the door closed behind me.

My car was sitting in the driveway, just the way I had left it, although it was looking grubby and needed a wash, but that was the least of my worries. I didn't even know when I would be back out on the road again with the top down and all.

I already had my keys in my hand and was inside in a matter of seconds. I stood still and listened, savouring the sound of nothing - complete silence, it was wonderful; no old people snoring, no machines beeping and no squeaking feet, just the fantastic sound of nothing.

I lived in a two-bedroom cottage in the country - alone - but that's the way I liked it. I made the choice to move out here alone, away from the hustle and bustle of the busy city life. And who doesn't like the country, anyway? I liked grabbing my camera whenever I felt like it, going for walks and taking photographs in the woods.

I was a portrait photographer back in the city, but I decided to pack it in and move out here for a change. And let me tell you, shooting landscapes is a whole different ball game, though just as much fun, nonetheless. I picked up my first camera when I was twelve and never looked back.

For me, there is something magical about capturing an image; freezing a moment in time. They say you can capture a person's soul in a photograph. I don't know if there is any truth behind that, but I like the idea.

3

I fell asleep as soon as my head hit the pillow that night. There was nothing more comforting in the world than being home and surrounded by my own things again. I slept the whole night through without waking.

It was a sharp shooting pain in my chest that promptly brought me back to the land of the living.

I grabbed at my chest, I was sure something was wrong, but the pain passed quickly. Nothing like the fear of a heart attack to wake you up in the morning, I thought. Harper had said I would be very tender for a while, so I figured that's what I was experiencing - tenderness. I got a little fright, I must admit.

I got out of bed and made my way into the bathroom. When I looked at myself in the mirror, I was almost convinced that I had aged ten years or more. I looked rough. My skin was a greyish colour and my eyes were a little bloodshot, not to mention a generous growth on my cheeks and chin.

I took a razor and some shaving gel from the mirrored cabinet above the sink. I lathered up my face and proceeded to eliminate the hair from my skin, with long gritty strokes of the razor. Ten minutes later and I was looking better already.

I opened my dressing gown and there it was, the permanent reminder of surgery. I stood there and stared at it in the mirror for a few moments. The scars were thick and raised and not yet fully healed. I hung my dressing gown on the back of the door and climbed into the shower.

Cold water crashed out of the shower and burst onto my head, a welcome invigorating sting. It took a minute or two for the water to run warm and it was nice when it did. I stood there for a long time with my eyes closed and my head slung back, just thinking, before I began to wash.

I climbed out of the shower and dried myself off. The mirror was all fogged up with steam. I rubbed it down with the corner of my towel.

Only an hour ago I had looked like a tired old man, but now, with a shave and a shower, I was looking and feeling much better. Ah, the simple things in life, I thought.

The heat from the shower had also helped loosen me up a bit, which was good. I headed back into my room and got dressed. It had been a while since I had donned anything more than pyjamas and revealing hospital robes. I pulled on a charcoal knitted jumper and a pair of black chinos, slid on my shoes and made my way downstairs. I was hungry and looking forward to breakfast.

There was next to nothing in the cupboards, they were almost bare. There was a lot of different kinds of pasta, but no sauce. I had been in hospital for several weeks, what else did I expect? The grocery fairies to stock the place up for me coming home? I realised I would have to venture out into the world sooner than I wanted to. That was my only option.

I wasn't feeling too excited about getting in the car and driving, but it had to be done. I told myself it may do me good. The nearest supermarket was about twenty minutes away, so the drive was fairly short and would ease me back into the swing of things nicely, I thought.

It was a gloomy day and I suspected it would be cold outside, so I pulled on a parka, then grabbed my keys and left.

Don't get me wrong, I love driving, though I was just a little anxious about getting back behind the wheel. I think I was scared in case I took a heart attack and swerved off the road and died, or worse, put someone else in danger.

I loved my car, maybe as much as a mother loves a child. And I'm not lying either. I used to drive an old banged up Citreon, mostly because I couldn't afford anything else. When I came into the money, I invested in something a little more elegant. I bought a Porsche 911 Cabriolet in an outstanding metallic burgundy colour. You could even say it was my dream car. I remember the day I bought it.

I got some funny looks when I walked into the showroom; they thought I couldn't afford to be there, but I quickly proved them wrong. All of a sudden it was 'Mr' this and 'Mr' that. It's funny how having money can change the way people perceive you.

I drove the car home that day with the top down. And there was nothing better than driving with the sun beating down on me, my hair blowing in the wind; sadly I don't have as much hair as I used to and that feeling will soon be a thing of the past.

Today it was too cold to drive with the top down. I was right about the weather, it was ice-cold outside. I quickly opened the door, jumped in and switched on the ignition. My baby came to life, humming; it was like a beautiful melody, vibrating in my ears.

I backed out of the driveway slowly and then pulled away, down the winding country roads, disappearing into the wilderness, surrounded by tall hanging trees.

The drive was rather relaxing and the roads were quiet which was a bonus. Driving a car is much like riding a bike, you never forget how to do it once you have learned.

I got to the supermarket

faster than I thought and didn't spend much time inside. I picked up all I would need for the next week or so and some much anticipated luxuries.

The drive home took a fair bit longer as the traffic had begun to pick up. Just before I got there something strange happened.

The only way I can describe what I was feeling is a fuzzy sensation in my right hand. Then my chest became itchy. I scratched at it lightly, but it was as if the itch was on the inside and it was more than irritating, let me tell you.

I pulled into the driveway and parked up. I retrieved my shopping and went in to the house. By this point my hand had started to become numb. I dumped the bags on the kitchen counter and then made my way upstairs into the bathroom.

When I pulled up my jumper and looked at my chest, there was nothing abnormal going on, the scar looked the same way it had earlier that morning. And that's when I started to experience some sort of craving.

It was almost like that feeling when you think you

have forgotten something, but more like I needed to do something. I was frustrated because I hadn't the slightest idea as to what that might be. The more frustrated I got, the stranger my hand started to feel.

I went downstairs and sat on the couch in the lounge and closed my eyes. However, all I could see was a bright red colour; it was a strange sensation, as though someone was shining a red light on my eyes. I sat there for five minutes, before the annoying itch in my chest began to ease off and the feeling in my hand started to come back. I decided it must have something to do with the medication Harper had put me on and then tried to forget about it.

Looking back now, I realise that was the beginning of the madness which would soon consume my life, like grey clouds blocking out the sun in the sky.

4

By now you are probably thinking about that all important question? You are thinking about the money and where it came from? It's funny, most people's ears stand to attention at the mention of the much loved dominator.

It's not the most exciting story in the world, I didn't

win the lottery. I didn’t win on a Lucky 7 scratch card, and I certainly didn’t rob a bank.

In fact, I came into money in the saddest way you can imagine. I inherited it. I'm not going to tell you how much, but let's just say I won't ever be begging for change on the streets.

You see, my old Grandma Pearl was a hard worker, a lawyer. She started at the age of twenty-five and was soon a high-profile defence lawyer. By the time she reached thirty-five, she was running her own law firm which quickly became very well established.

My Grandma Pearl never seemed to spend her money on much other than fancy suits and earrings. People around her were always speculating about where it all went, why she had never seemed to do anything with it. What was the point in doing all that hard work? You know, that kind of stuff. Others seemed to have better ways to spend HER money. I guess she was just dedicated to her work and never really got round to reaping the rewards.

Grandma Pearl died at eighty-two, which I would say

was a fair age for a woman who smoked like there was no tomorrow; at least forty a day, I'd say. Maybe it was the stress of her chosen career.

I was very close to her and was devastated when she passed away. I had seen her only two weeks before and she seemed her usual chirpy self. She died of a brain haemorrhage.

After her death, the vultures swooped in. By that, I mean my family, the family who no longer speak to me, none of them at all. I'm not too bothered about it if I'm honest. The last time I saw any of them was the day of the will reading.

They were all sitting there, anxious to find out how much they were going to get. I was the only one feeling the sadness of the occasion, crying my eyes out like a child. What happened next shocked me as much as everyone else in the room, even the lawyer who read out the will:

I have sat here for hours thinking long and hard about what I am going to do with my wealth. First let me say that I have taken every single aspect into consideration. I do not want my hard work to be squandered, I want my money to go to someone who will spend it wisely, someone who needs it and can do good with it. Most of all I want it to go to someone who truly loved me.

I hereby sign all of my finances over to my beloved Grandson, Charlie Finch.

Dream big my boy.

Pearl G. Finch.

I took a deep breath and tried to speak, but I couldn't. My life had just been transformed in a split second. I suppose that's all it takes, just one second.

I can remember the look on my mother's face, pure disgust, hatred even. My sister looked at me in much the same way. My dad gritted his teeth and shook his head in disbelief as he wrapped his arms around mum, now crying tears of frustration. As he helped her from the room, he snarled at me,

"You don't deserve it"

I didn't reply. I haven't seen them since. That was a year ago now. They couldn't even visit me in hospital. That's why I was so grateful to have met Alice.

It's funny how money can have the power to change people, to tear a family apart. Greed will be the death of us all. Mark my words.

The lawyer sat there in silence for a moment as he

watched my parents and my sister hurry from his office. He then looked at me and smiled broadly, pulling out some papers from his drawer, "I guess you'd better sign here then young man."

I did and then I left. I can't say that I wasn't a little bit happy, I'd be lying otherwise, but in that moment I would have traded all the money in the world for just a little more time with my Grandma Pearl. I'll never forget those words she wrote, dream big my boy.

5

Six weeks had passed since I had left the hospital and I must say, I was feeling pretty good. I could move a little faster. My body still ached, but not too badly. We were into November and it was beginning to get bitter cold outside. This was my favourite time of the year. I enjoy walking in the woods amongst the bare, skeletal trees. I like the feel of the frosty leaves crunching under my feet. The air is always crisp and fresh. I could tell the snow was on its way.

I walked out in the woods for hours, in an attempt to keep my strength up. It was a good way to exercise as it wasn't too strenuous. I also liked to explore, taking different routes on every venture. And of course, I always had my camera at the ready, just in case I came across anything interesting.

Most of the time I enjoyed being out in the woods alone.

Other times I wished there was someone to talk to. It was at these times that I thought about Alice, and how nice it would be to walk with her, have endless conversations about anything and everything.

I imagined taking her portrait in winter, amongst the trees, maybe even with some snow on the ground. That thought always made me smile.

We had traded details, but she had not yet contacted me. The last time I had talked to her was in the hospital before she went home. I had sat down on many occasions and written her lengthy emails. But I never sent them. I hoped that she would call me first. I didn't want to be the one to act first, for fear of seeming too needy.

One day, after a long walk, I decided to look through the photos I had just taken. I turned on my laptop, clicked open my emails. I felt a surge of excitement shoot through me when I saw that I had one new, unread email. Every part of me wished it was from Alice - but it wasn't. I didn't recognise the sender. Not that it was even a name, just a letter, **D**.

I scratched my head for a

moment - it could just be spam mail. Curiosity got the better of me however, and I clicked it open. There was nothing too exciting - there was nothing much at all actually, just one word in bold capitals, **STAY**. I admit it was bizarre, and I was puzzled, but I didn't think much of it and guessed it was some kind of technical error. Then I forgot all about it.

I took the memory card out of my camera and popped it into the card reader on my computer and waited for the 'bing bong'. As I was waiting on my photographs to load, I started to feel rather odd.

My eyes suddenly became itchy and fuzzy, almost like pins and needles. That is the best way to describe it. My vision became distorted and grainy, and I started to get a little dizzy. I raised up my left hand and put it over my eyes. Just as my hand made contact with my face, I experienced the sharpest pain shooting from my forehead, straight back to the nape of my neck. The pain only lasted for a split second. I thought that was it - until almost exactly one minute later, it happened again. And it kept on happening like that for about five minutes or so. I was scared to move and flinched in pain with every shot, my brain was on fire. And then the pain stopped suddenly. My vision became clear again and everything was back to normal.

I sat there in complete silence for a few moments, puzzled and scared. What the hell was going on? Just to be on the safe side, I decided to phone the hospital. I bashed in the number and listened to the ringing in my ear for a few moments before a girl with a high pitched voice answered. After a million questions and a million answers, she finally put me through to another line and I talked with a doctor.

He could put my mind at ease, saying that one of the side effects of my medication was headaches and he assured me they would calm down when my body got used to the drug. I sighed with relief when I hung up the phone, happy that there was nothing seriously wrong going on.

I decided to get away from the computer and rest my eyes. I left my bedroom and made my way downstairs and into the kitchen. I took a large glass from the cupboard, grabbed the milk from the fridge and filled the glass to the top. I drank it down in one and then poured myself another glass and went into the living room.

I turned on the television to see if there was anything on worth watching. When the screen came to life the original War of the Worlds was just starting, so I sat down on the sofa, put my feet up on the coffee table and relaxed with my glass of milk.

I hadn't seen much of the film when I fell asleep. When I woke up, the place was in darkness and the end credits were still rolling on the screen. I had spilled my milk all over myself. I looked over at the clock on the wall and it was only just past 7pm.

I decided it would be a good idea to get into bed early and have a long rest, with the hope of feeling better in the morning. And that's when I heard a strange noise coming from the hallway. I sat and listened for a moment before standing up. The noise was a continuous beeping sound.

As I made my way through the living room and into the hall the sound grew louder and louder. It was dark so I switched on the light.

As the light illuminated the hallway, the mystery was solved.

Somehow the telephone had made its way from the corner table where it sat and onto the floor. The handset was free from the cradle and the beeping was the sound of the receiver, which was pretty much phone talk for 'I will keep on beeping until you return me to my cradle'.

There is no way the phone could have just fallen over by itself and there was also nothing that could have interfered with the phone to make it do so. I felt a little shiver creeping up from the base of my spine. I bent over and picked up the phone and returned it to where it belonged. I switched off the television, changed into my pyjamas and then went to bed. But I lay there awake for a while before falling asleep, thinking about the phone on the floor.

I slept the whole night through without waking. When I opened my eyes, I was feeling fresh and my mind was clear. I got out of bed and slid on my slippers and dressing gown.

At the top of the stairs I could hear the beeping once

again. And as I descended down into the hall, there it was; the phone beeping away on the floor. There was no explanation and it was too early in the morning for me to try and think of one. I picked it up and, for the second time in the last twenty four hours, put it back where it belonged. I was a self confessed sceptic, but even I had no idea how it got there.

In the kitchen I poured myself a large bowl of muesli. I added some fresh grapes and low fat milk, then sat down at the table and began to eat. The cereal was dry and tasted like cardboard, but I was trying to stay fit and healthy. The grapes took the edge off at least, adding a little dash of flavour now and again.

I had only been sitting down for a few minutes when the craving and itching in my chest began, followed by the pins and needles in my eyes and the shooting pains in my head. This time there was a new addition to all the strange sensations and pains. There was an abundance of coloured shapes floating around in my eyes. The most prominent shape was square and yellow. I tried taking a few deep breaths in through my nose and out through my mouth, but it didn't help. I stood up.

I don't know why, but something guided me over to the kitchen drawers and I pulled one open. Although my vision was distorted, I could make out the shape of a notepad inside. I picked it up and then rustled around until I felt a pen in my hand, the pain shooting through my head making me wince every few moments.

I shuffled back over to the table and sat down, hoping

that what I had now come to call an 'episode' would pass quickly. I pulled open the pad and started scribbling. I didn't know what I was scribbling, but it actually took my mind off the pains in my head and the itching in my chest. For some unknown reason, scribbling began to put me at ease and within a few moments the episode had passed and the craving was gone.

I was glad it had been brief, more glad that it was over. When I looked down at the notepad, I hadn't created a masterpiece, which was not surprising. What I had in fact drawn was a shaky resemblance to the shapes I had seen floating around in my eyes. I had scribbled a few circles and a triangle, though the biggest shape on the page was a rectangle. I had added seven thick vertical lines inside.

The whole thing was peculiar and I couldn't think of a reason why such scribbling would have helped, but it did. That's all I know, it did.

I pushed the notepad aside and finished my breakfast. I needed to get out, get some fresh air. So as soon as I was washed and dressed, I grabbed my camera, pulled on my jacket and left.

6

From my house you can either turn left, right or walk straight over the road and into the woods. I tend to walk straight and over the road, but that day I took a left.

There is a small wooden fence at the side of my driveway. A while back I added a little gate in the middle. It creaked as I walked through it and I made a mental note to oil it at some point. Beyond the gate there was a muddy path which soon disappeared into the trees.

I love walking in the morning, the air always feels fresher. I never seemed to have anything important to hurry home for, so I just took my time, taking it all in. The wilderness does something to me, it inspires me. I always seem to think more clearly when I am freely wandering around, surrounded by nature. I think it may be down to the sound of the birds and the trees swaying gently above my head. It’s calming.

After walking for about fifteen minutes, I came across a track I had never seen before. I was surprised and a little excited to have found a new route. That Robert Frost poem popped into my head, the one about the road not taken. I smiled to myself as I ventured into new territory.

I felt as though I had stumbled into a magical land. The grass looked greener, the trees taller. This part of the woods seemed silent and untouched. To be fair, I don't usually see many people walking about. Sometimes there's a man walking his dog or a couple holding hands, but that's about it. So the likelihood is that not many people actually had come down this route before. I felt privileged.

As I walked deeper into the woods it got darker; there was little light coming in through the trees. I hadn't seen much wildlife and had spent my time taking photographs of trees and plants - nothing too exciting. That was until I came across this thick holly bush, which was absolutely covered in cobwebs, it was wonderful. The webs were all frosty and covered in dew drops; a little icy spider kingdom, I thought.

I spent a few moments photographing the webs before giving a light tap with my finger to see if I could entice a spider to come out and investigate. I was surprised when, after the second tap, one crept out from the mass of webbing.

It was one of those spiders with really small bodies and big, long hairy legs. I crouched down slowly, finally resting on my knees. The cold earth chilled my bones, but I ignored it; there was a fantastic photograph to be had.

I rustled in my bag for a moment, pulled out a macro lens and I got in as close as I could. The spider was just sitting there, still as a stone. Maybe he was posing for me. I got the shot, the spider's eyes big, black and shiny, with the frosty webs blurred out in the background.

I was about to take another backup shot when something caught the corner of my eye. All I can remember was a quick flash of something moving through the trees. My initial thought was that it may have been a dog, or a deer, so I quickly got to my feet and followed whatever it was, deeper into the woods.

I walked as quickly as I could. I would have run if I were in better health, but that was out of the question. My eyes were flickering all over the place, scanning the trees to see if I could find what I was looking for, but the woods were still, silent. The only sound was my feet crunching the leaves and the occasional twig cracking underfoot.

My body was beginning to ache, so I headed home. When I walked through the creaky gate and into my driveway, I could see that my front door was halfway open. I stopped breathing for a second and my body tensed. My initial thought was that someone was in the process of robbing my house. As I approached my door with caution, I tried to rationalise and think logically. I could have left it open by mistake.

I pushed the door slowly, still standing on the front steps. I looked down the hallway and listened. I took the camera from around my neck and wrapped the strap around my fist. If there was an intruder inside, a camera to the back of the head would make a good weapon.

I couldn't hear anything out of the ordinary, in fact, all I could hear was my own breathing. I placed a foot inside the doorway and then slowly made my way down the hallway, the camera at the ready in my hand, swinging by my right side. I peered through the crack in the door to the living room. There was nobody there - nobody forcing my flat screen television into their back pocket or anything like that.

I moved on through the living room and into the kitchen. Again there was nobody there. At this point I was almost certain that it was my own stupid mistake and I must have left the door ajar. But just to be on the safe side, I walked back into the hallway and up the stairs.

My bedroom was just the way I had left it and the spare bedroom was also untouched. I looked in the cupboards and under the beds, the way a kid does, looking for the bogey man, and there was still nothing. I walked down the hallway and into the bathroom and yet again, there was nobody stealing my soap and hand towels.

I stood there smiling at myself in the mirror, thinking, you are such a big paranoid kid. I even laughed out loud, although it was a short lived laugh. I fell silent suddenly. I could see my reflection in the mirror and I looked scared and pale. Something didn't feel right.

Something was wrong, I could sense it in my gut.

There was a sudden sound of movement coming from downstairs, the sound of someone running with haste and then a huge 'BANG!' as the front door slammed shut. I was frozen in the one position and it took a while for my feet to defrost and kick into action.

When they finally did, I dashed down the stairs as fast as I was able. Just before I got to the bottom of the steps my eyes started to become fuzzy; it was the start of another episode. Why now? I asked myself, now of all times.

I got to the bottom of the stairs, sliding on the flooring for a second. I steadied myself. The keys were swinging in the keyhole. I pulled the door open as quickly as I could. At that point I just wanted to put a face to the intruder. The main thing that freaked me out was the fact that I didn't know who it was.

I ran out into the garden, past my car, to the bottom of the driveway. I could still see, but only partially as the episode was beginning to take over. I surveyed the area, and for a second I thought I could see no-one. And then I looked over to the other side of the road.

I couldn't make out any prominent features. All I could see was the silhouette of a figure. The figure was really tall which made me conclude that it was most likely a male.

The only other thing that I noticed was that the figure was all dressed in black, and may well have been wearing some kind of trilby style hat. I only had a few seconds before it disappeared into the woods. I got the feeling he'd turned his head and stared at me, but I wasn't certain. A chill ran through me, right to my very core. Who was this stranger, and what did he want with me?

A few more seconds passed and then the episode went to town on me, full swing. My head was thumping and all I could see was a fuzzy landscape in the distance. I breathed in through my nose, and out through my mouth to try and calm myself. It wasn't working. I had to get inside. I had to draw.

I felt my way around, thinking to myself that the

car was my first safe point. If I could reach out and touch it, I would then be able to guide myself from there and back into the house. After stumbling around a bit, I finally felt the rear wing and more importantly, my bearings. I leaned against it and shimmied along the side doors. From there, I found the front steps. There were four of them. I counted my way up and into the house.

I closed the door behind me and twisted the key, twice, to double lock it. The pains in my head were excruciating, I stood for a few seconds to try and relax. My hand was now tingling, going numb. The craving was also getting worse.

I managed to get through the living room and into the kitchen. I felt around on the table until I found the notepad and the pen I had used earlier. I pulled the lid off the pen with my teeth and spat it out. I was becoming frantic, the pain was intolerable. I needed it to stop.

I rustled around with the pad and then began to draw. My hand seemed to be attracted to the paper, as though the pad was a magnet, my hand the metal. I started to scribble like before, although this time it was more scattered, it felt as though I was scribing a zigzagged pattern. The rectangle was still the most prominent thing in my mind, but the zigzagging was coming close to taking over.

The episode lasted longer than any others, almost twice as long, before it began to ease off. I felt lethargic and sick, my mouth was dry, my palms sweaty. I was so glad my vision was back and the pains in my head were gone.

I looked down at the notepad

to see what I had scribbled. I was right about the rectangle, it was the main shape on the page. I had gone over it a million times, so much so that the paper had begun to rip through to the next page. Definitely a rectangle, I thought. And again, I had scribed something inside the rectangle. This time it was different.

Before, I had drawn seven vertical lines. This time I had done only six. I had replaced the first line with a zigzag shape. I went over it a lot and it was rough, but it still resembled the letter

'M'.

I had no idea if there was any significance behind what I was drawing, all I knew was that it helped me feel better. That was good enough for me. I couldn't fathom why. Surely this wasn't one of the side effects of the pills. Harper's voice popped into my head,

"Now, Mr Finch, these pills are very powerful. They may well turn you into a paranoid, schizophrenic artist with a rectangle fetish, if you are not careful."

I imagined him standing there, shaking the box like a pack of Tic-Tacs. The thought made me smile. And for a moment I had completely forgotten about the figure on the other side of the road.

7

I didn't sleep a wink that night. Not a single one. I went to bed around nine, placing my notepad and pen under my pillow, just in case.

I just lay there in the gloom, staring at the ceiling, going over all the crazy stuff that had been happening lately in my head. I was sure part of me was going insane, if not all of me. The thoughts smashed around in my head, like fruit in a blender, eventually becoming all mashed and mixed to a pulp. And then I would start again from the beginning, solid thoughts, pulp, solid thoughts, pulp, all through the night. The time passed so slowly. Every time I looked at my clock, no more than one minute had ticked by.

After hours of lying there thinking, I felt like a zombie, the numbers from my digital clock etched into my retinas. Eventually, the sun started to come up and pierce through a crack in the curtains. I was glad it was morning, it made me feel more at ease. It was only 7:30am, much too early to get up; but what use was lying in bed doing nothing and driving myself crazy? I decided to get into a shower and waken myself up.

As I got to my feet, I looked over at my laptop on my desk and decided to have a quick look at my emails. As I had expected, there was nothing new. I went into the bathroom.

The shower had little effect. I knew I was going to

have a lazy day. I couldn't even be bothered getting dressed in proper clothes, so I just slipped into a pair of fresh linen pyjamas and pulled on a red woollen cardigan. It was rather chilly.

I made coffee and sat in front of the television. The programmes at that time in the morning are diabolical. These talk shows about sixteen year old girls getting pregnant by forty year old friends of the family really drive me crazy. It was either that or the 24 hour news channel, which makes me feel depressed. They run the same stories over and over again. Watching too much news almost makes me scared to go outside, hence I avoid it.

My host for the morning was some boring English guy with a bad haircut who liked to say 'put something on the end of it'. He was in love with himself, and his own voice for that matter, the narcissistic old bastard.

I finished my coffee then sat there, staring ahead in a trance. Soon the voice of the host became nothing but a drone. And then my eyes became heavy. Before I knew it I zonked out on the couch, drifting into a deep sleep.

I had a very vivid and terrifyingly real dream.

I was in the hospital again. Everything was as it had happened, as if I was reliving my past. But it wasn't me. It was as though I was watching myself in a film, and I knew every single thing that was going to happen next. Almost as if I had memorised the script for an audition.

I could move around freely, filling the role of head camera man. I had a God-like view of everything.

It was the morning of the operation and I was looking at myself watching old Bill in his bed. I then followed myself into the bathroom and saw myself changing into my new pyjamas and then back out of the bathroom and into bed. I admired the pretty nurse as she entered the ward to take me to theatre. I hadn't really noticed her beauty before, possibly because I was too nervous to think much about anything.

I then left that scene and turned and walked over to old Bill. I could still hear my own voice in the background and the sound of the pretty nurse as we conversed. I became entranced by Bill's eyes. I leaned in closer to have a better look. And that's when they changed. His eyes turned completely black for a second before returning to normal. They were like glass and I could see myself in the reflection. He then started going crazy.

He was looking right at me. Right into my soul. Screaming and pointing, he looked terrified. Could he really see me? Was I really there? Am I here? I asked myself as I jumped back. The nurse ran into the room with the needle. My heart began to pound uncontrollably. I ran back to my bed and whispered into my own ear,

'Wake up, Charlie, we need to get out of here. Something isn't right.'

It was no good. All I could do was observe.

We walked down the corridors to theatre where the surgeons talked in their own foreign language. Just before the anaesthetist placed the mask over my face, I walked over to the edge of the bed and shouted at myself, 'Don't fall asleep! We can't fall asleep! We can't leave the time line, Charlie!'

It was no good. I drifted off

like I knew I would. It had already happened, after all.

8

A loud ringing noise sucked me out of my dream. I shot up, awake in an instant. I sat for a few seconds, as still as I could. I was groggy because I had jumped up so fast. Maybe it was in my dream, I thought. A few moments passed. I was a little disoriented, unsure what time of day it was. Maybe I had slept all through the day and into the night? It was a possibility.

I looked over at the living room blinds, I hadn't opened them when I got up in the morning. It seemed dull outside, though not quite dark. I guessed it was early afternoon, maybe three or four.

As I was looking over, a shadow moved across the blind. My heart sank as I quickly remembered the intruder. Was it him, had he come back?

I got to my feet as quietly as I could and made my way into the kitchen. I pulled a knife from the rack on the counter. I dropped the blade with a clatter as the shadow rapped on my window. I knelt down and picked it up, the handle cold in my hand. I noticed it tremble. My heart was racing and I had that sick feeling of dread in my gut.

I had to go out there. I had to confront my tormentor. I had to put a face to this mysterious figure.

I took a deep breath and walked down the hallway to the front door. I stopped for a few seconds, taking another deep breath, before twisting the keys and pulling the door open with force. I was brandishing the knife, swinging it around this way and that like a mad man as I shouted,

"Who are you and what do you want! Leave me alone!"

And then suddenly I was silent, in shock. The knife fell to the floor with a metallic thud. I knew the face staring up at me, for I had seen it before.

I can remember when I was a kid I had this weird obsession with becoming an astronaut. I can't remember how it all came about, I can just remember telling my dad that I wanted to stand on the stars and gaze upon Jupiter and Saturn and Mars and all the other planets. His reply was,

"What are you, some kind of a faggot? You'd better not grow up and turn out to be a queer! Just my luck, my only son turns out to be a queer, Jesus, could you imagine that?"

I never mentioned it again; but that didn't stop me from constantly thinking about it, dreaming about it. I was ten years old and I wanted to be an astronaut. The funny thing is, at that age I actually believed I would achieve the dream.

I was fascinated with the thought of being up there in space all alone, gazing down on earth. I made up scenarios in my head, where I would always end up being some kind of a hero who went the extra mile to save the day. I would be on television sets all over the world, audiences glued to the news coverage, amazed at my bravery.

In those news reports, there would be a montage showing how I was just a normal guy, leading an ordinary life; just a normal guy, with an extraordinary ambition. And then, boom, cut to footage of me saving the day in space. It's funny how things turn out.

You get to fifteen. The dream is still there, but it's fading. Twenty. You could still make it. By the time you hit twenty-six, however, the dream is almost a distant memory. That's when you realise, you *are* just a normal guy, leading a normal life. A normal guy, with no extraordinary ambition. Just another robot amongst the billions.

Yet I have never been able to shake the feeling that I was here for a reason, almost as if I was meant to do something. I just never figured out what that *something* was.

I stood at my front door, absolutely speechless. I tried to say something, anything, but nothing would come out. The cold air hit me. And it took me a few moments to realise that everything was white. My car looked invisible under a thick blanket of fresh velvet snow.

"You okay there, Charlie? You scared the shit outta me!" the voice said,

"You look like you just seen a ghost."

I hadn't slept well, my episodes were getting worse,

there had been someone in my house and I didn't know who. I was a frail mess, my mind all shot to shit. I was expecting something terrible to happen when I opened the door. Now, I was relieved. Shocked but relieved. I stood there for another few moments, taking it all in, calming myself down.

The snow was still falling, it was beautiful. A few flakes hit my face every couple of seconds and melted on my skin, which was refreshing. I snapped out of it and looked down. And there she was. Her hair all covered in snow, her little red nose, her sweet lips. The shadow outside my window was Alice. She was looking up at me, confused, staring at me like some kind of a lunatic.

I was standing in my doorway, a lengthy kitchen knife at my feet, wearing a pair of linen pyjamas and a red woollen cardigan. I felt like a fool, a complete and utter fool. I gathered my thoughts.

"What are you doing here?" I asked.

"Well it's nice to see you too."

"I'm sorry, I'm just a little shocked to see you, that's

all."

"Do you know how many emails I've sent you? A reply would have been nice, you know?"

I was confused.

"What emails? I've checked a million times and all I've had is spam mail."

"Well I can assure you, Charlie, I emailed you almost ten times, not to mention the phone calls. I was getting worried because you never replied, so I figured I'd drive out here and see if you were okay."

Alice squinted her eyes and then continued,

"To be perfectly honest with

you, you don't look too great. What's with all the shouting? And the knife?"

She had tried to contact me? I must have written down some wrong digits in my details, I thought.

"Look, I've not been feeling myself lately. You better come inside and get warmed up, I can explain."

A faint smile crossed her face.

"You aren't going to murder me in there with that thing, are you?" she said, pointing to the blade on the floor. I looked down and kicked it

aside. I felt a grin growing,
"Of course not, this isn't a Halloween movie you know. C'mon, I'll put the kettle on."
The snow crunched under her feet as she climbed the stairs.
"Nice outfit," she said. "Red really looks good on you."

The snow had begun to lessen as I looked out upon the dying day. I checked to the left and to the right, then across the road...there he was again, the dark stranger. I was sure he was staring back. I closed the door behind me and locked it twice.

9

I put the kettle on then grabbed two cups from the cupboard and set them on the counter. Alice was sitting on a chair by the kitchen table. Her eyes wandered for a few seconds before she said,

"Nice place you got."

"Thanks," I said, "I really like it out here."

The kettle clicked and I

poured the coffee. I placed a mug in front of Alice before sitting down myself, facing her from across the table. I looked at her and smiled.

"It's real nice to see you, Charlie. You had me worried." She hardly knows me and she's worried? That must be a good sign, I can remember thinking.

"I'm happy to see you too." I could feel the butterflies beginning to stir in my stomach. My face was feeling a little on the hot side and I hoped I hadn't turned red to match my cardigan.

"So what was the deal with the knife?"

She quizzed.

I wanted to make up some kind of a lie, but I was never a great liar in my time. I always found it better to go for the truth. So I thought for a second in my head, before trying to explain my frantic outbreak.

"Well," I took a breath, "I think it started when I was walking in the woods the other day."

She looked puzzled. That too was a thought I had just had in the second before I started explaining.

"What is 'it'?"

"I was in the woods taking some photographs when something caught the corner of my eye."

"And?"

"And I followed whatever it was. I thought it might have been a deer or something like that, so I hurried through the woods to try and see. At first I thought it might have been a photo opportunity, but then I think I just became curious and wanted to find out what it was. I never found out."

Alice sat there, looking even more confused. She took a sip of coffee, peering at me above the mug, listening intently.

"After that I decided to call it a day and walked home. Then as I got here, I noticed my front door was open."

"Couldn't you just have forgotten to lock it yourself when you left the house?" she said.

"That's the thing. I thought that myself at first. When I got inside, I had a look around. There was nothing missing and nobody inside. Then I went upstairs just to make sure and there wasn't anybody up there either." She laughed at me.

"Are you sure YOU haven't

been watching too many scary movies?"

She could see that I wasn't laughing, then continued,

"Why do you look so edgy?"

"Well, I even laughed at myself at first. But when I was upstairs, suddenly something didn't feel right. I felt scared. And then there was this sound."

"What kind of sound?"

"It sounded like someone running down the hallway and then the door banged shut."

Alice now had a serious look on her face, more stern, concerned even.

"So what was it? The sound?"

I decided it wouldn't be lying to leave part of the story out. I didn't want her to feel unsafe in my house or freak her.

"I'm not too sure, and that's why I'm so on edge."

I really wasn't too sure what was going on, and that *was* the truth.

"Strange. Let's be rational though. Maybe you did, in fact, leave the door open when you left. And then the sound was the wind catching in the hallway, forcing the door to slam?"

"Maybe you are right. I probably just need a good

sleep and a long lie in bed."

"I'm sure you'll be right as rain in the morning." she said.

"Yeah."

But she hadn't seen what I had seen. She hadn't seen *him* at the other side of the road. And he had come back again. The thought of him standing there made the nape of my neck tingle.

"Anyway," I said, "tell me about you and what you've been doing with yourself."

And just like that, we changed the subject. Soon, I became drunk on the sound of her voice flowing into my ears.

10

I woke up on the sofa, it was already morning. I couldn't even remember falling asleep. Alice had her head on my lap and she was still sleeping. I didn't want to move in case I woke her, so I savoured the moment and just admired her.

She looked so peaceful and innocent. Her eyes flickered every now and then and it looked as though she was smiling, which made my heart melt.

As I observed her every breath and her petite figure, I wondered how old she was. I was sure she was younger than me, maybe twenty-six? Or maybe she was forty and had just aged well. You know what they say, never ask a woman her age.

I had never been in love, never really had a long term relationship, if I am entirely honest. I was feeling something I had never felt before. Is it possible to fall in love with someone you hardly know? Does love at first sight exist?

I must have drifted off to sleep again. This time when I woke up, Alice wasn't there. I felt a sadness building and for a moment I hated my head for making me dream that she was. She was so real, I thought. She seemed so *real*.

I convinced myself that I was actually losing my marbles, that was until I smelled something. Something like bacon. Then I heard something. Someone happily humming away to herself. I walked into the kitchen and all my sadness vanished. Alice was cooking breakfast.

She looked over her shoulder and smiled at me, her eyes sparkling.

"I hope you don't mind," she said.

"Let me tell you, nobody has ever cooked breakfast here but me. Badly, may I add. It's nice to see someone else doing the hard work for a change."

She laughed. I was getting used to saying things that made her laugh. It made me feel good.

"Well, a man needs a good breakfast in the morning to set him up for the day."

"If you insist. I'm not going

to argue with you," I replied.

"So, after breakfast we are going a walk, okay?"

The winter portrait of her that I had often thought about on my walks was the first thing to pop into my head. It was even snowing outside, just the way I had imagined it.

"Sounds like a plan."

I really must make the most of it before she goes home, I thought.

I wasn't really supposed to be eating fatty foods, doctor's orders, but I told myself that once in a while a treat was okay. There were only six rashers in a pack anyway, what was the harm?

I sat down at the table, happy as a pig in shit. Then I knew it was all too good to be true. Within seconds, an episode started to take hold of me. Fuck, how am I going to play this? Alice was already plating up.

"Just a minute," I said.

"You okay?"

"Yeah, just forgot to take my pills. I'll be back in a minute."

"Okay, hurry or else your breakfast will get cold."

I dashed up the stairs and into my bedroom, closing the door behind me. I fumbled around under my pillow and pulled out my notebook and pen and the scribbling started once again. I was beginning to control the episodes much better, even the scribbling was becoming more like actual sketching.

Only minutes later, it was over. When I looked down at the paper, I now had four characters within the rectangle, one letter and three numbers - M713. Was I totally nuts and solving some kind of a code like fucking Rainman? Those characters meant nothing to me.

Alice called something from

the kitchen, I'm not sure what.

"Just a second," I shouted, replacing the notebook and pen.

I walked into the kitchen; bacon, French toast and sautéed mushrooms. It looked fantastic. Not a lot of people know this, but food truly is the best way to a man's heart.

Alice was already sitting at the table and she had made a pot of fresh coffee. I poured us both a cup and tucked in to breakfast. It was even better than it looked.

"This is great," I said.

"I know," she replied, "I'm

pretty good in the kitchen, you know."

"Amen to that," I said, "Amen to that."

As we left the house later, I looked over the road. The snow was now thicker than it had been and it was a little foggy, but I was sure there was no one there. I hadn't noticed the night before, that Alice's car was parked right at the bottom of the driveway. I couldn't tell what kind it was, just that it had to be extremely small; it was barely visible in the snow.

We were all wrapped up in our winter gear. Well, when I say our, I mean *my*. Alice was wearing one of my old parka jackets, which was very roomy on her, and a pair of mittens, which were also too big. Fashion doesn't really matter out here, it's not as though anyone would see us dressed like abominable snowmen.

She looked adorable. We crunched through the snow, passed through the creaky gate to the left and disappeared into the white winter landscape.

Everything seemed different, covered in snow; like a completely different land altogether, actually. The trees were all blanketed in a sheet of white. Every now and then, massive clumps would fall from the branches high above and we would need to dive aside.

We walked for a long time, just talking and taking it all in and it was lovely. I enjoyed having company for a change. I snapped some photos of trees and things, though that winter portrait was never far from my mind.

One thing about taking

portraits - people are all natural and beautiful until the camera pops up, and as soon as that lens is aimed in their direction, they become all squint-eyed and sour-faced. Imitating Quasimodo, I'm sad to say.

After about an hour or so, we approached a row of trees which created a kind of gigantic archway. Alice was a good few feet in front of me, talking away. I had come to realise that she loved to talk, a lot. That was fine with me.

"Stop," I said.

She turned around and looked

at me.

"What is it?" she asked.

"Can I shoot your portrait?"

"Me? Why? I doubt I'd make a nice photograph."

A shy reply, I thought. I'm sure she blushed but I can't be totally certain as her cheeks were already red from the cold.

"Humour me?" I asked.

"Okay, fine. So what do I have to do, where will I stand?"

"Just stand right where you are and be yourself."

"Okay."

I walked in a little closer and framed from her head to

just under her chin.

"You know what, pull up the hood," I instructed. The fur arched round her head perfectly. She had a faint smile on her face, though it was fading.

"Is this okay?" she asked.

I took the shot without replying and she didn't go all squint-eyed or sour-faced. I could tell it was golden.

'Chimping' is one thing I do not do and I even hate to see other people doing it. But I had to see right there and then what it looked like.

I knew in an instant that it was the most beautiful

portrait I had ever taken; the most perfectly composed, the most elegant and, importantly, the most natural.

And in that moment, I also realised that I had in fact fallen in love with someone I barely knew.

"Let me see," she said.

"No, no, no," I replied, "an artist never shows his work until it is complete."

"Let me see," she pleaded, running over and trying to pull the camera out of my hand. We then did that penguin thing again, you know, like I talked about before? Anyway, we danced around for a few seconds, before our eyes locked.

Time seemed to freeze and I kind of wish it had done. I would have quite happily stayed there forever, until the end of days. I'm not too sure what happened next, if I made the first move or Alice did. Her cold plump lips pushed hard against mine. Electricity shot through me. If I was dreaming, I wanted to sleep for the rest of my life. We walked home, hand in hand, everything was perfect.

I had never really been able to trust anyone in my life, but I trusted Alice. I trusted that she was genuine. And I guess if she wasn't, she couldn't really break my heart - my heart was already broken in a furnace somewhere.

11

When we got home, we went inside and put the kettle on. We were frozen to the core, though I wasn't really that bothered, if I'm honest. All I cared about was the fact that she was here, with me.

While Alice was making coffee, I went upstairs and set my camera on my desk and then turned on my computer and inserted the memory card into the reader.

The photos were taking a while to load up, so I decided to check my mail. There were three new unread emails waiting in my inbox. They were from three different senders and like before, the messages were not sent from a name, just letters - **B, M, B**.

I clicked open the first message from 'B'. Again, there was only one word in bold capitals - **AWAY**. I still couldn't understood where these messages were coming from. They still didn't make sense. I clicked open the message from 'M'.

Again, one word in bold capitals - **MAN**. So far I had 'AWAY MAN' which seemed like absolute word vomit. I was convinced it was some kind of marketing scheme that was going to have some big grand finisher, so I clicked open the third and final message from 'B'.

When I read it, I just about stopped breathing and died on the spot. My palms became sweaty and I could feel beads of moisture instantly forming on my brow. There were three bold words this time - **IN BLACK HAT!**

Now it was all beginning to make sense. I scrolled back to the very first message I had received from 'D'. I had forgotten what it said.

Someone was fucking with me. I didn't know who or why, but whoever it was, they were out to get me. I clicked open the first message and then pieced all four messages together.

STAY

AWAY

MAN

IN BLACK HAT!

This was linked to the intruder, surely. I remember

thinking he was wearing a hat of some kind. What the fuck was happening to me? I sat back and ran my hand through my hair and then cupped it on the back of my neck, just staring at the screen, and just at that, a new message popped up, this time the sender was blank.

I was becoming more and more terrified. Was my mind beginning to attack itself? Creating things that were not real? Was Alice ACTUALLY in my kitchen making coffee? I just didn't know any more. I had to read the next message.

In block capitals, there was

more word vomit which didn't make even an ounce of sense -

FUZZ PULL

FUZZ PULL

CRACKLE FUZZ PULL

SWORD KNIFE

DEATH LIFE

CRACKLE FUZZ PULL!

Like I said, not one ounce of sense. And then the most bizarre and unnerving thing happened.

As I was trying to take in all the madness and make sense of what was going on and thinking about who it was that was trying to spook me, my camera fired off by itself. The camera was close and it blinded me for a moment or two.

When the blindness had worn off, I picked it up from my desk. The camera was off which would make it impossible to misfire. I clicked it on, my thumb hovering over the triangle playback button next to the d-pad on the back.

All of a sudden I felt calm. A familiar scent entered the air. I knew the smell but I just couldn't place it. I was sure it was musk, like the perfume older women wear. I clicked the playback button.

I should have been hysterical, I should have shot up out of my chair and run a million miles, but I didn't. What I did feel was some kind of comfort, protection even. I didn't look my best in the photo that appeared on the LCD screen, I'll admit that, though she did.

She was standing right behind me with her hands on my shoulders with a peaceful smile on her face. She was wearing a blue dressing gown, just the way I remembered her when I was little. It was as though she was actually there in the photo.

I turned around and there was nobody there but me, but a moment later, I felt something soft brushing over the back of my hand, as though a feather had just floated down and tickled me on the way by, although there was no feather. I knew it was my grandma Pearl.

I looked back at the photo on the screen and her face had changed from happy to concerned. Then she began to move within the photo. I know it sounds crazy, but she did, I swear to God, she did. She raised one hand and pointed over at my bed; as she did, my craving began. It was time again and I knew what I had to do.

I stood up and walked over to my bed. I was just about to put my hand under the pillow to get my notebook and pen, when the notebook slid out from under the pillow all by itself. The pages then flicked open to a fresh blank page. The pen shot up and I caught it. I began to draw, and then everything became black.

D B M B (Dream Big My Boy)

When I woke up in the morning, I was tucked up in bed. I couldn't remember getting there, I couldn't remember much of anything if I'm honest. It was bright and my mouth was like cotton. I rolled to my left and Alice was in bed next to me. She was lying there just staring.

"Hey, sleepy head," she said.

"What happened?" I asked.

"You came upstairs when I was making coffee and you fell asleep. You must have been exhausted."

"Really?"

"Yeah. How are you feeling this morning?"

I rubbed my hand down my chest and then stretched out.

"You know what, I'm actually feeling really good. Refreshed and dandy."

"Good. I'm glad."

She had a look of excitement on her face.

"Why do you look so happy?" I asked.

"Well, I'm in bed with you for starters."

My stomach began to dance.

"And second?" I quizzed.

"Well, I know you are a photographer. But you didn't

tell me you were an artist too!" she said.

"What do you mean?" I asked. She pulled out my notebook from under the bed and my guts began to churn. Now I would have to explain the episodes.

Alice flicked to the centre of the notebook to show me a picture I cannot remember drawing. It was a portrait of a man. Quite a handsome man, though he looked sad. There was a rectangle at the bottom of the drawing, perfectly straight lines and all. There were now seven characters within the rectangle - M713 RAB.

I was confused and couldn't remember drawing the picture. Although I could remember the first four characters within the rectangle. The portrait was probably the most perfect portrait I have ever seen, done with only berol pen. Did I really draw that, I thought?

"This is fabulous, Charlie." Alice was excited.

"Thanks."

I played along.

"You know, I always wanted to meet a real artist."

"Well...um, yeah. Now you have."

She rolled over and kissed me, a shiver ran through me, right to my groin.

"Guess what we are going to do today?"

I was dreading to think what she was going to come out with.

"What's that then?"

"Well, we are going to redo this drawing with paints on a canvas, fancy that?"

I knew it was a bad idea, but I wanted to make her happy. I couldn't ever imagine seeing a sad look on her face. I would have pretty much done anything she asked me, even if that meant shitting bricks and spewing glass.

"Sounds great." I said.

"One more thing."

"Yeah?"

"Why did you sign the drawing as," she squinted her eyes as she pulled up the notebook to her face,

"Mr. Frank Denver?"

Who was Frank Denver? I thought. The first thing that popped into my head was,

"It's the title."

That wasn't a lie, because I had obviously drawn the damned thing when I was trapped in an episode. We got out of bed, got dressed, and headed into town. I could feel a horrible vibe. I knew something bad was approaching.

12

I had never painted a day in my life and now I was walking around some artsy-fartsy place pretending I was an artist. I was almost beginning to believe it, for I seemed to know a lot about different paints and brushes and canvas sizes. I must have watched a documentary and stored it in my mind somewhere, I thought.

Some guy in a terrible spew-coloured jumper came over and asked us if we were okay and I just looked at him and said,

"Yes, we are fine. I am an artist you know?"

"I didn't know that sir."

His coarse voice didn't fit his young face. As he walked away he said,

"You came to the right place."

I picked up a variety of acrylic paints in all different colours, some brushes and a rather large canvas.

"I can't wait to see you in action!" Alice exclaimed.

I just smiled but felt sick inside. What if I couldn't do it? Would a mash of paint on a canvas pass me off as an abstract artist? She wanted a portrait and I was going to have to try my best to give her what she wanted.

We walked over to the till, paid and then left. As we got in the car, I started to feel extremely sick and dizzy. I tried to push it off, but I couldn't. I kicked the car door open and was violently sick, onto the street.

"God, Charlie, you okay?" Alice said as she rubbed my back.

I took a few moments to compose myself and then grumbled,

"Yeah, must have been something I ate."

"Look, let me drive us home and get you into bed."

"Okay, that would be good." I said.

We got out of the car and switched sides and then she pulled away. I had never let anyone else drive my baby before and I must admit I was reluctant to do so. But there was no way I could have driven.

I threw my head back and tried to relax, but I could

feel more vomit creeping up from my guts. There was also a pain in my chest which was beginning to throb, mildly at first but getting increasingly worse. After another five minutes of driving I could hardly hold it.

"We're going to have to pull over at the next rest point. I need a bathroom."

"Hold on, there's one up ahead. You don't look great Charlie, you look grey."

About a mile later we pulled in at a service station. Luckily they had a bathroom. I flew out the door and ran to it as fast as I could.

I was on my knees in an instant and chucking my guts up into the pan. I was there for a good ten minutes in that dingy cubicle. In that time, I noticed some bad graffiti on the cubicle wall, "The DEVIL made me do it."

I spewed some more. I thought it was never going to end. All of a sudden, I heard someone whistling. I hadn't heard anyone else enter the bathroom, but someone was definitely there.

"You okay in there?"

It was a male voice and he must have been talking to me; I was the only other person there.

"Yeah, fine, thanks."

"Who are you trying to kid?"

"Just a bit of food poisoning, that's all. Honestly."

"You know it's starting to reject? You know that, right?"

If you have ever had a conversation through a door whilst trying to keep your entire stomach from exiting your mouth, you will understand my difficulty.

"What do you mean?"

"That old heart of yours, it's rejecting. I'd say you have a month, if that."

I froze solid, hanging on to

the pan. The taps behind the door splashed on and then he continued to whistle something I had never heard before.

"Who are you? How'd you know..."

He cut me off.

"I know more than YOU know. I know you want to live and spend some more time with that pretty little thing of yours who is waiting on you outside in that big fancy car."

I wiped my mouth and stood up. How did this person know so much, about me, about Alice?

"Who are you?"

He ignored me and continued, "How are those doodles of yours coming along?"

My chest was aching and my legs were becoming weaker and weaker. I was getting dizzy.

"How do you know about that?"

"I know a lot of things. I also know that you shouldn't be messing about with things you don't understand. It will get you in trouble."

I had to see what this guy looked like. I had to put a face to the voice. I took a few deep breaths and tried to hold back being sick for a minute, then pushed open the cubicle door.

He was standing right there waiting on me. He looked different than I had expected, I'm not sure how exactly, just different. He was all dressed in black and wearing an emerald green tie which was embossed with a floral design. And on his head, he was wearing a black trilby hat.

I knew in an instant that he was the intruder, the dark stranger at the other side of the road. I was scared, of course I was scared. But I was also too weak and too ill to care.

"Why were you in my house? What do you want?"

My eyes were drifting in and out of focus.

"Don't be alarmed, dear Charlie. Think of me as a... guardian angel, if you will?"

"Just tell me what you want?"

"You don't have to be scared of me. My name is Calder Gunn. I'm here to help you, that's all. Everyone needs a little help sometime."

"I don't need your help."

"Oh, but you will, in time."

"Just leave me alone."

Everything started getting brighter and brighter. Then there was a buzzing sound in my ears. I fell to the ground with a thud and then everything went white.

The overhead fluorescent light was flickering. For a second I didn't know where I was. I was on my back on the floor and there was a strong stench of urine. It took me a while to remember that I was in the bathroom. I no longer felt sick. I actually felt pretty good. How long had I been lying there? I didn't know. I had to get out. I had to make sure Alice was okay. I sprang to my feet, washed my face and hands at the sink and then hurried outside.

I ran over to my car. Alice was still inside. She had fallen asleep, slumped over the wheel. I tapped on the driver's window gently and she jumped. She was a little startled for a minute, then she opened the passenger door and I climbed in next to her. She threw her hands around me and gave me a big kiss on the cheek.

"You don't smell too good," she said.

"I know. I've probably smelled better."

Alice smiled.

"How are you feeling now?"

"Strangely enough, I actually feel pretty good. I must have gotten it all out of my system."

"Are you sure you are okay? I was worried."

"I'm sure. Let's go home."

I pulled on my seat-belt. Alice started the engine and soon we were back on the road.

13

We got home around 3:00pm. I calculated from the time that I was only lying on the bathroom floor for about ten minutes. I couldn't get Calder Gunn out of my head. What kind of a name was that anyway? How did he know so much about me and my life? I headed into the shower to clean myself up.

I thought about the messages

my Grandma Pearl had left me. She had warned me *Stay away man in black hat*, but I was intrigued and weirdly drawn to this Gunn character. If what he was saying was true, then I only had one month left to live. Could I really take that chance? What if he wasn't just a crack-pot? He knew things about me that he couldn't possibly have had access to. I had an unexplainable feeling inside which made me think he was telling the truth.

I climbed out of the shower and got into my pyjamas and then made my way downstairs. Alice was sitting on the sofa and she wolf whistled at me as I walked into the living room.

The canvas was set up on an easel in the corner of the room, ready and waiting for me. I wasn't up to it. Maybe I should just spill and tell her all about the episodes and my encounter with Gunn? I quickly decided against that option.

"Hey, do you want to cuddle up with me and watch a movie?" I asked her.

"Don't you want to paint?"

"I'm not really feeling any inspiration at the minute. I'd rather cuddle up with you and watch a movie."

"That sounds lovely." she

said.

"You can chose the movie," I told her, and she did.

Her choice was John Carpenter's The Thing, which I thought was a very good choice indeed. We got comfortable. I stroked her hair and nuzzled into her neck. This was bliss and I never wanted it to end. If this Gunn fella was telling the truth, it would be coming to an end sooner than I'd anticipated.

We watched the movie, although I wasn't really paying attention. I was focusing more on the sound of Alice breathing, the feel of her skin against mine. I knew the story off by heart anyway, I'd seen it a million times before.

We went to bed pretty early that night and after making love, Alice fell asleep. I couldn't. My mind was too active. The most active it had been in a long time, actually. I had a particularly stupid thought and I went with it. Now, looking back, I really wish I hadn't.

I slowly got out of bed, quietly got dressed and slid on my shoes. I gave Alice a gentle kiss on the head before going downstairs. I pulled on my jacket, picked up my car keys and then left, locking the door behind me.

As I drove down the country roads, I wondered what the fuck I was doing. I had left a beautiful woman alone in bed, what was I thinking? There was only one thing on my mind, and although I didn't want to admit it, I already knew where I was heading. I had to see Gunn. I needed to talk to him with a clear mind.

14

I pulled up outside the service station. I still wasn't sure what the hell I was doing there, but I wanted to find Gunn.

The whole place was in darkness. Don't service stations stay open 24 hours these days? Then I thought about how the world we live in is horrible and stopped blaming the service station attendant for not being there. Just a light in the all night box would have made me feel better.

There was a static sound in the air and the windows in the car steamed up. Something told me to get out. I walked over the gravel and stood next to a petrol pump. This is stupid, I thought. And just as I was about to get back in my car, I heard his voice,

"Well, well. You showed up sooner than I expected."

I turned to face him and he had a large grin stretching from one ear to the other.

"You knew I'd come?"

"I knew you would at some point, yes. They always do."

"What does that mean? What do you want from me?"

"Never mind, Charlie. Like I said, I'm here to help you."

"How do I know you aren't just spouting me a whole load of lies? How do I know what you said about my heart rejecting is true?"

"You don't have to take my word for it. I can show you."

I was a little baffled. He slowly walked towards me. I was uneasy but curiosity was getting the better of me.

"Now," he said, "Deep breaths

in, long breaths out."

I did what he said. He slowly reached out and placed one hand at each side of my head. I thought for a moment he was going to snap my neck, but luckily he didn't. Instead, he told me to close my eyes.

As soon as I did, all I could see was a mass of bright flashing lights and I couldn't hear a thing. It was uncomfortable and making me feel sick. I tried to open my eyes, but couldn't.

The flashing lights were intense and colourful at first, though after a few moments they started to calm down and then materialise into images. I can't fully describe what it was like as I have never experienced anything so surreal in my life. If I had to, I would say it was like a dream, but I knew I was actually there. My mind had just been transported to another time. It sounds crazy, but that's how it was.

I was sitting in a wheelchair and I looked frail and sick. My skin was the colour of ash and my eyes vacant, just like old Bill's. The way I never wanted to end up. I was at home, Alice was there. She was on the phone in the kitchen and she was crying uncontrollably. I couldn't hear what she was saying, though she looked horribly upset.

There was more vivid flashing and then a new scene materialised. I was in the back of an ambulance. Alice was looking down on me and holding my hand. Again, she was saying something but I didn’t know what. The tears in her eyes looked so real, as if I could reach out and wipe them away. I wish I could have, but I was too weak.

Another sequence of

colourful flashing materialised into the third and final scene. I was at my own funeral, just lying there in an open casket as stiff as a stone, looking out but unable to move my eyes. Again, Alice was there, looking down on me. Something was different about her. After she had said her goodbyes and kissed me on the forehead, she walked away. That's when I noticed, from the corner of my eye, that she was pregnant. I tried to scream, reach out after her, but it was useless, she was gone.

Everything went black for a

moment and then there was a nasty ringing in my ears.

"Follow my voice and open your eyes," the voice said. It sounded flat at first, but it grew louder and louder until finally, my eyes shot open. I was panting uncontrollably and I was sweating like a mad man.

"What the fuck did you do to me?" I yelled.

"Charlie, my dear boy, I just showed you the future."

"Everything seemed so...REAL."

"That's because it was."

"How did you do that? How can you possibly know my fate?"

"Some questions don't need answers, Charlie. The question you should be asking is how to alter your future."

He said it with a look of childish excitement in his deep dark eyes.

"And this is the part where you tell me you can 'help' me?" I replied.

"Yes, exactly. Now you're beginning to get the hang of it."

"So...you help me and I get to live?"

When I said those words out loud, I realised it sounded insane. However, I couldn't deny the fact that Gunn had done something God-like to me. Why shouldn't I believe him? He had shown me my future.

"You got it in one, Charlie my boy."

I weighed up the pros and cons. Let's just say this is real for a minute, I thought. If I were going to die in a month, like this guy said, he could apparently stop it from happening and I could live happily ever after. If I get in my car and go home, I may only have a month left to live. I concluded that I had nothing to lose and everything to gain.

"So how does this work? You

do whatever magic it is you do and I pay you? Because the money isn't a problem."

"No. I don't want your money. I just want to help you."

"Okay then, can you help me?" He clapped his hands and bellowed.

"I thought you would never ask!"

He fumbled around excitedly in his jacket pocket for a few seconds before producing a silver hip flask. It had his name inscribed on the front. I found that a little strange and rather narcissistic. I looked past the flask, wondering what was inside.

"What's in the flask?"

"The elixir of life, my dear boy."

"Are you telling me if I drink from that flask, I'll live?"

"Yes. Oh yes. You will live and so much more, Charlie."

"Nothing to lose," I thought, as I took the flask from his long skeletal hands.

"Bottoms up." I said as I took a healthy swig.

I was expecting some kind of spirit, but it was thick like oil and tasted disgusting. I could feel it slowly rolling down my body. That's when it began to burn. The pain was excruciating. I clawed at my chest and my throat. Gunn was loving it, he was standing there cheering and clapping. Everything was high-pitched and the sound was hurting my brain. That's the last thing I remember, before falling to my knees. Then everything went white.

15

The first thing I remember seeing when I came round was the ceiling. There was a sun beam piercing through the window, over my face. The warmth was nice. I could tell it was morning as the birds were happily singing outside. I was confused and it took me a few seconds to realise I was not in my own bedroom, or my own bed for that matter. I was, in fact, lying on my back on the living room floor. I couldn't remember getting there. Then I thought about my spontaneous trip to the service station and a cold chill started to stir under my flesh.

I quickly sat up. There were a million and one thoughts buzzing around in my head. Everything seemed more vivid and clear to me, even the white paint on the ceiling. I sat staring at it for a few moments; it was really something.

I got to my feet expecting every bone in my body to be aching after spending the night on the hard floor, but there were no aches and no pains whatsoever. I felt fit and healthy, like a twenty year old athlete. Even the ache in my chest had vanished.

I slowly walked over to the corner of the room and admired the painting as though I was an art expert. It was a fine piece of art, too. I would go as far to say it was perfect, flawless to the very last stroke. I couldn't remember painting the portrait, but I looked down and my hands were covered in paint.

The painting was a complete replica of the small berol portrait I had sketched, but in full colour and a thousand times bigger - it was huge. Once again I had signed the painting as Mr. Frank Denver.

The massive face on the canvas was staring back at me. It looked so real that I almost expected him to start talking to me. He looked sad and his eyes were a little glazed. This Mr. Frank Denver definitely had had some sorrow in his life, I thought.

I had the feeling I knew him, though I had never seen

him in my life before. Could I have passed this guy in the street and pulled him out of my subconscious? It was a plausible explanation.

There was paint everywhere and four or five different sized brushes lying around. The most prominent colour on the canvas was red. There was also a lot of yellow, but red was definitely the statement colour.

The floorboards creaked behind me. I turned around and Alice was standing in the doorway, wide-eyed and open-mouthed.

"I am speechless, I...this

must have taken you all night?"

It was show-time.

"Yeah, I couldn't sleep, so I decided to get up and make a start. Then I just couldn't stop and ended up losing track of time." I replied.

I was beginning to form a real talent for manipulating the truth. For the truth was, I couldn't remember doing the painting at all. Not a single stroke of a brush, nothing.

"It is amazing, Charlie! I feel as though he is standing right there, it's so realistic. The eyes look so... human," Alice said as she wrapped her arms around me.

"Who is he?" she asked.

"I'm not too sure. I think I must have made him up in my head."

"You could sell your work to an art dealer, have you ever thought about doing that?" she asked.

"No, I don't want to make money from it, that takes away the enjoyment of creating art in the first place. Art shouldn't be a source of income, it should be a source of fulfilment and expression."

I shocked myself with that reply. It just flowed out of my mouth ready-made, not like my own way of speaking. I sounded like a real artist.

"Well it's up to you, my love, but I reckon you could have work like this hanging in a gallery somewhere, being admired by thousands of people."

"Thank you," I smiled, "That means a lot to me."

Alice looked up at me, "You are one-in-a-million Charlie. I love you," she said and then kissed me on the lips. Butterflies started to dance in my stomach, electricity shot through my body in steady waves.

"I love you too Alice, more

than anything in the world. I knew I loved you the first minute I set eyes on you."

Her little face went red as she kissed me on the lips once again.

After breakfast we decided we would go for a nice long walk in the woods. I went upstairs to shower. I let the water run for a few minutes while I got undressed. I then got the shock of my life.

As I looked at myself in the mirror, the first thing I noticed was that I looked a little younger, not much, but it was noticeable. There weren't as many wrinkles on my face. My skin was more radiant and fresh. My hair was thicker. I couldn't explain it, but I definitely had a healthier head of hair than I had had just the day before. All these things were impossible, but as I looked down I was staring at something beyond impossible. My skin began to prickle.

The scar on my chest had simply vanished. There was not a single mark left on me. It was as though I had never been through surgery and that couldn't be. I can remember everything; the hospital, Old

Bill, the pain, meeting Alice, it was all real and it had all happened.

Something was very wrong. I was scared and confused. There was no explanation. I had to hide it from Alice; she would think I was some kind of freak and there were no words I could say to make her understand. I couldn't even understand it myself. But it was real and it was happening.

I closed my eyes so tight it hurt and tried to concentrate hard. This had to be a dream and if I stayed calm and concentrated on waking up, I would. I opened my eyes and I was still standing there naked in front of the mirror. My hair was still thicker, I was still younger and my scar had still vanished.

I showered as quickly as I could then went into my bedroom to get dressed. I pulled on a shirt with lightning speed and buttoned it up, all the way to the top. I slid into my trousers and put on my shoes and tied the laces with ease.

Alice appeared at the top of the stairs.

"You got ready quickly." she said.

I just smiled at her as she

smiled back.

Alice walked into the bathroom and her voice faded behind the door, "I won't be too long."

I knew she would be, she always took forever to get ready, but I didn't mind. I had a feeling there was something I had to do.

I hurried downstairs as soon as I heard Alice turn on the shower. I pulled a large white table cloth out from the kitchen cupboard and went into the living room. The face in the painting was staring at me, taunting me.

"Shut the hell up!"
I muttered to myself.

I laid the table cloth on the floor then grabbed the painting from the easel and placed it face down on the cloth and wrapped it up. There was a foul stench in the air and a familiar static sound in my ears. I tried to ignore it. I hadn't much time.

As I picked up the painting my guts began to churn. There was a faint voice in my head. I wasn't too sure if it was my own or someone else's.

"Go!" the voice demanded, "Go, now!"

I grabbed my car keys from

the table and left the house, locking the door behind me, leaving Alice alone and oblivious. I climbed into my car, placing the painting in the passenger seat. The engine roared to life. I skidded out of the driveway and was gone in an instant.

16

I can't tell you where I was going, because I didn’t know myself. I just had the strongest feeling that I had to be somewhere. There seemed to be something guiding me to my final destination. Maybe it was a higher power or maybe I had developed some kind of second sight. Maybe I'll never know.

I kept driving without thinking, turning when it felt right. And after about half an hour or so, I felt as though I was where I was supposed to be. My stomach swirled and I could hear my heart beating faster and faster...and the voice inside my head,

"Go now," it said, "Number 32."

As I looked to my left, I could see a row of houses. I was driving past number 16, so I slowed down and crawled along the road at snail's pace.

16, 18, 20, 22, 24, 26, 28, 30...32.

I stopped the car. The house wasn't big or fancy, or different in any way, but I was drawn to it. Grubby windows looked as though they hadn't been washed in years, the splintered door with rusty numbers on it.

I stood on the street for a few moments, staring over at the house, before leaning in to the car and picking up the painting.

"Go, now!"

I wasn't sure what I was going to say if someone answered, but I walked up the driveway, the painting secure under my arm, and knocked on the door anyway. There was no answer so I knocked again. Still no answer.

A rational thought popped into my head, what the hell are you doing, have you lost your marbles?

I had convinced myself that I had to knock on this particular door but now I was convinced that it was time to leave and forget all about it, so I turned to walk away. Alice would be wondering where I was.

As I started walking away, I heard a key turning in the lock and then the door opening.

"Who the fuck are you? Why are you in my garden?"

The voice was not familiar to me and the tone was intimidating. I felt fear rising inside as I turned around to face the occupant of number 32.

He was young and handsome and he stared deep into my eyes, smoke dancing up his face from the cigarette hanging from his mouth. I was speechless. My hands began to shake.

"Are you deaf or something? What the fuck do you want?"

I was frozen stiff. The

world was spinning around me. All I could do was stand there and stare. I had completely forgotten about the canvas under my arm, and it was slipping away from me. I tried to grab it, but I was too slow and only caught the corner of the cloth.

It slid off quickly and the canvas fell to the ground. Landing face-up, my work of art was revealed to the man in the doorway. It was as though I had just performed a world-class magic trick and he was now the one rendered speechless.

"I'm sorry...I don't know why

I'm in your driveway. I had this feeling you see - "

He cut me off.

"What the fuck is that?" he said,

pointing to the ground.

"Look, I don't know, I swear. I just had this feeling that I had to come here. It's a long story."

"Why are you painting pictures of me? I've never met you before in my life!"

He had regained his voice and was now clearly baffled.

"I don't know. I have these 'episodes' and black out. It started as scribbles in a notepad, but it is getting more out of control. I painted this last night and I can't even remember doing it. Believe me, I am finding this just as weird as you."

"What kind of episodes?" he quizzed.

"I really can't explain, I'm sorry to bother you. I thought I could get some answers here."

"Well now I'm the one who wants answers, so you better start explaining this shit!"

"You'll think I'm crazy."

"I already do."

I had nothing to lose and I was already coming across as a mad man anyway. I figured he wouldn't believe my tale so I started at the beginning, but he soon became agitated with the details of the transplant and meeting Alice.

"Just cut to the painting!"

"Well, I met this creepy fella the other day who claimed he could help me." Concern swept over his face.

"What do you mean, help you?"

"He said my heart was going to reject and then he made me drink this stuff fro – "

"What did he look like?" he exclaimed.

"He was all dressed in black, green tie and a trilby hat." He was now chalk white,

"Gunn," he whispered.

"Yes," I said, "That was his name. Calder Gunn."

"You don't have any idea what you have gotten yourself into, do you?"

Those words put the fear of death into me.

"No. I'm guessing you are going to tell me though?"

"You are in for one hell of a fucking ride, let's just say that."

I wished in that moment that I had never got in the car, that I had never knocked on number 32. If I could have gone back in time and changed it, I would. Then the world has a peculiar way of working.

"I'm not sure what you mean? Can you help me?"

He ignored my question then flicked his cigarette out onto the grass.

I wanted to be home with Alice. I wanted to feel her skin on my mine, I wanted to hear those words flowing out from her lips 'I love you'.

"What is your name?" he asked.

"Charlie," I replied.

He reached out his hand and I shook it as he said,

"Frank, Frank Denver. You better pick up your little

finger painting and come inside."

I followed him into his house. This was just the beginning. The beginning of something bigger than you or me.

Art can only be had by the damned.

Charlie Finch.

END

THE RANCID SERIES CONTINUES...

PLITHORIAN

COMING SOON

Made in the USA
Charleston, SC
15 November 2015